Contents

Sss!
Focus: s, a, t, p as in <u>s</u>un, <u>a</u>dd, <u>t</u>ap, <u>p</u>en 3

Pat, pat!
Focus: s, a, t, p as in <u>s</u>un, <u>a</u>dd, <u>t</u>ap, <u>p</u>en 8

Phonemes: s a t p

About this book

These short stories are designed to give young children blending and reading practice. They are decodable, which means the words in them only include letter shapes and sounds that the children have learned. The stories also gradually introduce a few 'tricky' words, which are essential for children to become familiar with, such as 'they', 'of' and 'said'.

As children progress through these readers, new letter sounds and 'tricky' words are added and previous learning is revised. The progression links directly to the teaching order in the Letterland teaching range. Each story begins with a title page that provides information for children and teachers.

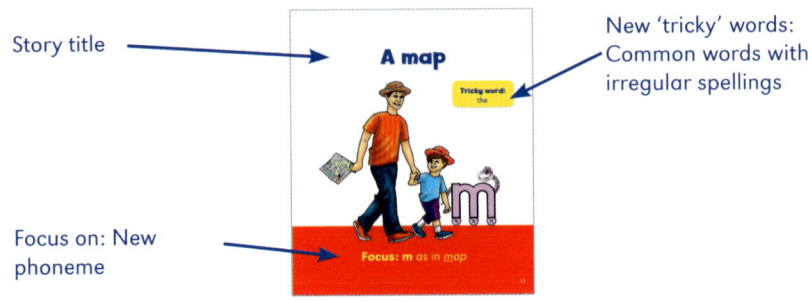

Teaching tips:

- Encourage the sounding out of the decodable words (and any decodable parts of 'tricky' words).
- Discuss the stories with the children to ensure comprehension and engagement.
- Encourage re-reading in pairs or individually to develop fluency and reading for meaning.

Sss!

Focus on: s, a, t, p

Sss...

Zzz...

Tap, tap, tap!

Sss!

Sss... a... t...

Sat.

Pat, pat!

Focus on: s, a, t, p

Sssss!

A, a!

T, t, t!

P, p, p! Pat, pat!

About this series

This series of 8 books accompanies the Letterland teaching range. Each book contains a selection of short stories, featuring the phonic elements listed below. In total there are 30 engaging stories that children can use to decode the 26 most regular alphabet sounds, as well as some 'tricky' high-frequency words.

Book	Focus elements	As in the word...	Story titles
1	s a t p	sun, add, tap, pen	Sss! Pat, pat!
2	s a t p i n m d	it, net, map, dog	Sit! Is it Nip? A map Nat is sad
3	s a t p i n m d g o c k	go, odd, cat, kit	Is it Dan? Tom and Tim Yes or no? Stop!
4	s a t p i n m d g o c k ck e u r	duck, egg, up, run	Can he kick? Is Ed a pet? Mop it up! Red Robot runs
5	s a t p i n m d g o c k ck e u r h b f l	hen, bat, fan, leg	A hat for a pet Ben and the cub Huff and puff Leg rest
6	s a t p i n m d g o c k ck e u r h b f l j v w x	jet, van, wig, box	Just jump! At the vet's Wet! Can he fix it?
7	s a t p i n m d g o c k ck e u r h b f l j v w x y z q ng	yes, zip, quiz, ring	Yo-yo Man's yams Zig, zag A quick quiz Ding, dong!
8	blends bl, cl, fl, gl, pl br, cr, dr, fr, gr, tr sk, sl, sm, sn, sp, st, sw	block, clock, flag, glad, plug brick, crab, drip, frog, grin track, skate, slip, smash snap, spot, stuck, swim	A robin on a clock Drip, drip, drop! It is hot! Skid, smack!

Collect the sets

Phonics Readers – Red Series

Phonics Readers – Blue Series

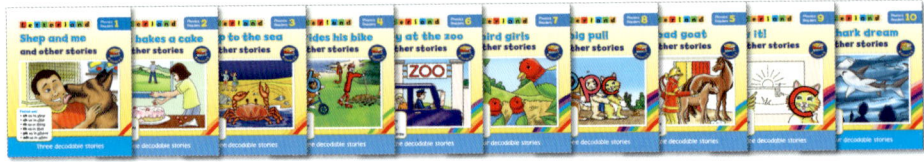

Published by Letterland International Ltd, Leatherhead, Surrey, KT22 9AD, UK
www.letterland.com
ISBN: 978-1-78248-172-0
Product Code: TH93

© Letterland International 2016
LETTERLAND® is a registered trademark of Lyn Wendon.

First published 2013. This new edition published 2016. Reprinted 2019.
10 9 8 7 6 5 4 3 2

Author: Lisa Holt
Originator of Letterland: Lyn Wendon
Artwork: Baz Rowell
Design: Lisa Holt

The author asserts the moral right to be identified as the author of this work. All rights reserved. No part of this publication may be reproduced, stored in a retrieval system, or transmitted in any form or by any means, electronic, mechanical, photocopying, recording or otherwise, without either the prior permission of the Publisher or a licence permitting restricted copying in the United Kingdom issued by the Copyright Licensing Agency Ltd, 90 Tottenham Court Road, London W1T 4LP. This book is sold subject to the condition that it shall not by way of trade or otherwise be lent, hired out or otherwise circulated without the Publisher's prior consent.

Printed in Turkey.